I0520449

Warlord of the

Saints

Peace on Earth

Episode 1

The Morning After

By Michael Sandoz

Otheneret Publications

Printed and bound in the UK by Amazon

ISBN-10: 1-911386-00-X
ISBN-13: 978-1-911386-00-1

DEDICATION

This Episode is dedicated to all those who have lost
their life unnecessarily to the Big C .

Let it not be in vain

Let us shield the pain

Let us stop and pause

Let us find the cause

I thank everyone who buys this episode and the ones that
follow. Half the profits of this book will go towards
finding the cause(s) of cancer.

Let's do it in our lifetime.

You might not like the answers that are found but, hey ho,
I am not here to entertain you, I am here to find the truth.

This episode is, however, here to entertain you.
Enjoy the story.

Series 1 of 3, Episode 1 of 10

**Front Cover Design by
Michael Sandoz**

CONTENTS

ACKNOWLEDGMENTS

I would just like to thank everyone I know for turning me into the person I am today.

A Pleb.

I apologize for the script writing, but the intention is to get a producer interested as early as possible so more charity money can be raised for "The Cause". Once the entire novel 'Peace on Earth' has been finished I will then put it together into a hardback novel.

I trust you understand, and enjoy the ride

Extracts from the Authorized Version of the Bible (The King James Bible), the rights in which are vested in the Crown, are reproduced by permission of the Crown's Patentee, Cambridge University Press

Warlord of the Saints
Series 1

Peace on Earth
(As it is in Heaven)

Episode 1

Prelude

Just to give you a head start with the names because it will get very confusing at times, most of the people in the story have at least three names, one real (in a fictional sense) and the rest nicknames.:-

Mickey aka St Michael — also answers to Wibble, Shorty, DB, but won't answer to Porg and has yet to accept Slattery. Other nicknames courted over the years and cited occasionally include Arnold, Magro, Magri, Charles, Aznavour, Rono and the much hated but thankfully forgotten Beany.

Steve Rickham answers to Chopper, Rick Rock and Stevie, but expect a thump.

Darrell Wood will respond to Dipper or Dip only (the explanation of such will become apparent much later in these episodes), and Chuckle Bear apparently, but not once to Lanky.

Martin Wilmot has been known to respond to Donny, Chimp and Unlucky.

Gus Barley the sensible solicitor will look up to Beavis, Derek Duvall, shortened to Dez, dezmond, dezmeister, Duvall, and Ted.

Kevin McClarry answers to Ted.

Calvin Barker, loves Eros, Omar, and any other names associating him with good lovers. Rommel has also been associated with him due to his dirty tricks campaign which is ongoing.

"The Twins", well what can I say about the twins, they are pretty much responsible for all the above nicknames and will answer as a combined unit to "the chicken shits", and singularly to anything, but they are generally called:-

Carl Kyte aka Tank, Chumpy, Kyteman, "The immature one". Chumpy incidentally is a phrase coined to identify the sort of girl who goes out dressed like her mom, and is slightly overweight, hence chubby frump…..…or Chump for short. What this has to do with Carl is anyone's guess.

Bob Kyte aka Fat Bob, Bobby, Clutch, Afro (short for Aphrokyte, nothing, may I add to do with him being a beautiful goddess, it just sounds funny saying Afro to a blonde Fat Bob). And just to put the record straight for the discerning reader, already thinking about putting the script down as it's not funny taking the mick out of fat people, he ain't actually fat, just slightly bigger than his brother.

Sometimes we mix the twins names up just to annoy the split eggs. (Daz's idea, wish I'd thought of that one).

May I finally add that this is not "The Hangover Part IV", and the majority of the goings on in this novel are incidents that have occurred in my lifetime, maybe not in the sequence of events to make this script flow, and not necessarily by the characters pertained in this novel but certainly witnessed by myself over the last 40 plus years. I will let you decide which ones didn't happen. It's not as easy as it sounds.

And finally just to set the record straight, these characters generally don't smoke, they don't even know where the cigarette machine is in the pub let alone the drugs baron, most of these events happened whilst under the influence of that extremely potent but legal class A+++ drug… alcohol.

Enjoy the read.

Synopsis

2016. Peace on Earth?

Revelation 13 - 4.

"And they worshipped the dragon which gave power unto the beast: and they worshipped the beast, saying, Who is like unto the beast? who is able to make war with him?"

-
-
-
-

The boys have embarked on a joint golfing birthday bash to Southport. But golf isn't on their minds.

One of their best mates is missing, but you can't have everything.

St Michael is on Earth but his alter ego Wibble is failing miserably to get through.

Michael seems to know rather a lot when under the influence to the entertainment of his mates, but when sober spends most of his time plotting the next practical joke.

Wibble is spouting is usual drivel after a gallon of lager, and the boys keep themselves entertained with their own view of it.

Then it all changes……….

It is the coming of the false prophet……

1

Series 1
Warlord of the Saints - Peace on Earth

1. Screenshot with biblical images   1

Scrolling text

2. Revelations Chapter 19   2
   verse 11.

'And I saw heaven opened, and behold a white horse; and he that sat upon him was called Faithful and True, and in righteousness he doth judge and make war.

'His eyes were as a flame of fire, and on his head were many crowns; and he had a name written, that no man knew, but he himself………..'

To fade….

Episode 1 The Morning After.

3. INT. Hotel Bedroom – 3
Morning   Fade in

DARRELL.'s phone starts ringing to the tune of 'wild boys'.

Daz is brought out of his slumber.

Whilst rolling off the base of the bed and rummaging through his pockets he scans the room in a state of utter horror.

Darrell.
(rather hung over and dishevelled).

Shorty, I think we've been robbed son

MICHAEL.

Huh, can't move Lanky, what's this on top of me?

Darrell.

It's the mattress mate, were you cold in the night?

Michael.
(panicking).

Arrrhh!.. get it off

As Daz removes the mattress he
starts chuckling.

Michael.
(sitting up and scratching
his privates through
his underpants).

This isn't the time for
laughter Dip

Darrell.

Check out the mirror
Porg, you appear to
have a double burger stuck
to the side of your mush

Michael.
(moving to the mirror and
peeling something green
and red off his cheek).

Errhh, what's that?

Darrell.

A gherkin one would
presume… with ketchup

Michael.
(taking a bite and
offering the leftovers).

Do you want some?

Darrell.

No ta Wib, I could eat a
scabby hoss out of Eros's
butt cheeks, but I couldn't
eat that….. it's been on
your face

Michael.
(finishing off the gherkin
and looking around slowly
and disbelievingly).

Very funny Lanky……wow, what
happened to the room
matey?, and what makes you
think we've been robbed?,
we seem to have gained a
few items

As the duo look around the bedroom
the full extent of the upheaval
becomes apparent. Shaving foam

covers the walls, a traffic cone sits on the TV, a hanging flower basket full of petunia's hangs from the central light, a pay as you go city bike props open the en-suite door, the hugely expensive oil painting that had the previous evening hung from the hotel reception wall is pride of place… stuck to the ceiling.

Darrell.
(rather bemused).

This ain't looking good Shorty

Michael.

You gone 'n put your interior design skills to use again Dip…. Arhhh Lanky, I see what you mean, yes your mattress is missing

Darrell.

No Wibble, my wallet's missing, what shall I do?

Michael.

Cancel your cards son asap......have you searched the room thoroughly?

Darrell.
(looking around the bedraggled boudoir).

Not exactly, but I did leave it in my jeans last night

Michael.
(sarcastically).

That's not good Dipper, there's circumstantial evidence someone's frequented our room, get on the dog and cancel 'em now

Darrell.
(picking up the phone which is dripping in sticky rum and coke).

Yes Sherlock, when I went to bed this place was spotless

Michael.

Ha ha ha ha ha!

Darrell.

Quieten down son, I'm
on to the bank

Michael.

Sorry Dip, I was just
thinking how darn lucky we
are

Darrell.

How?

Michael.

That there's no Bengal
tiger in the bathroom

Darrell.
**(smirking and in
an Indian accent).**

Called Richard Parker?

They both start laughing.

Darrell.
(shushing Mickey).

Yes it's bank
account number…..

Michael meanwhile is inquisitively
checking out the traffic cone.

Darrell.
(putting down the phone).

What's worse Porg, the
missus can't spend anything
now, I've just had to
cancel both our cards. I
couldn't remember if mine
was issue one or two?

Michael.
**(still inspecting the
cone).**

Couldn't think of anything
better….. they were
talented robbers Dip to
make this balance on the TV

Darrell.
**(walking over and prizing
the cone from the TV).**

Gum, and about six packs
judging by this mess,

Darrell. Cont'd.
(walking to the door).

Ohhh that's rank, but that smell's making me hungry, come on Porg let's go get some snap, and get that picture down off the ceiling Shorty, we need to get that back before they notice it's missing

Michael.
(staring up at the picture).

Funny Lanky…. very funny

Dip reaches up and prizes it down.

Darrell.

Yep, that rules you out of the equation Wib

Darrell. cont'd.
(turning the painting over and shaking his head).

More gum

Michael.
(pulling the evidence
out of the waste paper bin
and holding it up).

At least they had the
common decency to put
the wrapping paper in
the bin. So Daz, my
conclusions are.. we're
looking for a very tall,
bike riding, bubble
blowing, cleanly shaven
traffic cop with OCD,
and a penchant for fine
art

Darrell.
(punching the hanging
flower basket which falls
and hits the TV).

Who loves flower arranging,
and was in a desperate need
of a mattress

Daz moves the bike, Mickey
shuffles past and opens the
bedroom door.

The mystery of the missing
mattress then becomes apparent.

There on the landing is the offending mattress with duvet, pillow and a head poking out the top.

Daz and Mickey look at each other silently before Mickey cuts the air with a knife.

4. INT. Corridor/Bedroom   4
Door Morning Cont'd

Michael.

You know you're always saying you wouldn't kick her out of bed for farting Lanky?....

So what exactly did she do to deserve this?

Darrell.
(snapping his fingers, and reaching down to pull the quilt back).

KERChing… you ain't funny Porg, but I think this is a bloke not a lass

Michael.

Arh, batting for the other
side is treason Dipper?,

Darrell.

He wasn't in my…

Michael.

We'll have to get in touch
with Cadbury's to see if
they can create the
Bournville Boulevard
Dip..…the back door treat

Darrell.

Not listening Shorty, this
is Donny!

MARTIN sits up.

Martin.

Morning sweet peas

Darrell.
(rather authoritarian).

Are you the reason for
the rearranged deranged
bedroom son?

Martin.

(yawning).

Not me lads, it was like that when I crawled in at 05.30

Michael.

How'd you get in the room?

Martin.

Door was open

Darrell.

Why asleep on the landing, were you looking for passing trade?

Martin.

You two reprobates were snoring like an express train, Daz was on the floor, so I borrowed the mattress, alright?, look you can have it back, why the third degree?

Michael.

Daz's wallet's gone

Martin.

Ohhhh, must have been short
of leather, 'cause there's
usually fuck all else in it

Michael.

I had pondered, over to you
Dip?

Darrell.

Cheap, in my time of crisis
you go 'n punch me in the
gonads, I am offended,
quick Chimp, help me and
Wib back in with the
mattress before they charge
us for this additional room

Martin arises, completely and
utterly naked.

Michael.

Jees, where's your clothes
Donny?, so that's where the
nickname chimp comes from

Mickey reaches forward and strokes
his hairy arm.

Martin.

In your bath soaking wet,
had a wee accident

Darrell.

OK time out, why didn't
you just go back to your
own room?

Martin.
(rather forlorn).

Beavis wouldn't let me in

Michael.
(picking up the mattress)

I can fully understand that
Chimp, any brief in his
right mind wouldn't let you
anywhere near him, come on
Donny me lad help us with
this mattress and stick
some of Daz's clothes on
'cause they'll look funny
on you

> **Martin.**
> **(helping Mickey shuffle the mattress past the bike).**
>
> Careful with that bike Wib, I need to get my one pound deposit back on that

> **Darrell.**
> **(still in corridor).**
>
> That answers one more conundrum, hurry up a scabby hoss is awaiting downstairs and my belly wait's for no one

5. INT. Bottom of Stairs next to Reception. Cont'd.   5

Daz holds the other two back.

> **Darrell.**
>
> Right lads listen up, Chimp you go an' distract the receptionist by asking her to check the office PC for an email you are expecting and no chatting her up or small talk, as my stomach's rumbling...

Darrell. Cont'd.

And ma midriff has little patience, Wib.. you shimmy across the marble floor, hop across the desk, I'll throw the painting over to you which you hang and dart back across the desk.. capisce?

Michael.
(whispering).

Sounds like a plan Dip, off you go Chimp

As soon as the receptionist disappears into the office, Mickey sprints across the shiny floor, leaps over the desk catching his leg on the telephone cable and crashes into the back wall in a heap on the ground, Daz right behind him chucks the rather expensive oil canvas over the reception desk which lands on top of him, fortunately not tearing.

The receptionist comes back through the door to see what the kerfuffle is.

Receptionist.

Can I help you sir?

Michael.
(picking himself up).

Ermm... maintenance, thought I would go over the desk rather than wait for you to come back, caught my leg and kerplunk, was putting this painting back after it's spring clean, oh would you look at that.... no screws, just gunna go back to my van to get some screws, can you hold on to it whilst I'm gone, be careful not to damage it, it's a Bacon, won't be long

Mickey hands her the painting, opens the hatch and makes a sharp exit towards the revolving doors.

Martin.
(making a hasty retreat towards the breakfast lounge).

I'll come back later for my email, you look busy

6. INT. Breakfast Restaurant.   6
Cont'd

As Dipper and Donny enter the restaurant they are greeted by the boys already tucking into a full English.

CARL.
(younger twin).

Morning lads, good night's sleep?

BOB.
(older chubbier twin).

They'd sleep through a hurricane Chumpy

GUS and STEVE fall about laughing.

Darrell.

Not funny chaps, anyone had my wallet?

Steve.

Not me

Darrell.

Hmmm, I can cope with the "Hanging Gardens of Babylon" strung from the light, but the wallet is below the belt Chopper

Steve.

No, I wouldn't find that funny Dip, sure it hasn't dropped out of your pocket sometime during last night's capers?

Darrell.

Who knows?

7. EXT – Breakfast Restaurant Exit Doors.   7

Mickey Wibble bangs on the emergency exit doors looking for someone to let him in.

Steve.

Ahh, burger face arrives, let him in Beavis so long as he doesn't look to angry

Gus gets up and walks over to the doors.

Gus.
(at the exit doors).

What's wrong with the normal doors Wib?, always like to make an unconventional entrance don't you

Michael.
(walking over to the boys).

Let's just say it involves bacon Beavis, but not the sort I'm about to devour

Darrell.

Why didn't you let Donny in your room Beavis?

Gus.

No reason Daz, other than a gallon of loopy juice knocking me out, where's your card key Donny?

Martin.
(sheepishly).

Had it confiscated, I'm never going out with those twins again

Steve.

It's their 50th birthday bash, settle in for the long haul son, we have another two nights to go

Martin.
(under his breath whilst looking at the menu).

Thought you lot had grown up by now

Carl.
(inspecting Martins wrist).

Oooohhh.. that looks sore son?

**8. INT. Night Club Evening   8
(cut to evening scene whilst talking)**

Martin. VO.

No thanks to you Chumpy,

Martin. VO. Cont'd.

and your Fat Bob twin over
there, not easy getting
police grade cuffs off
whilst tied to a chick. She
wanted to go home at 11
sharp but she had to stay
with me till blue watch
turned up at 4am.

If I could've stopped her
getting agitated and trying
to run in the opposite
direction maybe my wrist
would be less on fire by
now

9. EXT – Breakfast Restaurant   9

Bob.

Serves you right, trying
to handcuff us twins
together was never going
to work was it?

Carl.

At least she wasn't a
minger Chimp

Martin.

Yeah but you tied my right
hand to her right hand
hence we were always
facing in the opposite
direction…. I didn't get
to see her mush much

Carl.

Cute base though

Gus breaks into song standing up
and twerking.

The boys nod approvingly.

Martin.

Back drafted a touch, I
suppose I do only have
myself to blame

Gus.
(sitting back down).

Who called the fire brigade
Donny?

Fade Across

**10.   EXT. Outside Night Club.   10
            Late Evening (Cut to
            scene whilst talking)**

Martin. (VO).

The chick, but things took
a turn for the worse when
her boyfriend turned up in
Denis on blue watch with
his squadron

Fade back

**11.   INT. Breakfast   11
            Restaurant.**

**Darrell.
(pulling a full turtle with
Mickey).**

O oh, this sounds messy

Michael.

Messier than a babies
nappy, Dipper

Steve.

Or your bedroom

12.   EXT. Outside Night Club   12
Late Previous Evening

Martin.(VO)

It was boys, it was,
fortunately he took it
all in good humour,
however after they sawed
off the cuffs they hosed me
down full force and now
I know what rioters feel
like when the police get
the water cannons out, I
hit the wall opposite
at quite a pace…………

They then confiscated
my room key…..

13.   INT. Breakfast Restaurant.   13

Michael.
(looking at Daz).

Ahhh, that explains the wet
clothes in the bath

Darrell.

I was rather hoping he
hadn't pishhed himself, I
can have a shower now

Carl.

Donny, didn't we leave
you with Calvin?

Martin.

Yeah Tank, but the girls
were both '*well into fire
fighter's*' and once her
friend found out Eros
was one as well they
shimmied off together,
with a parting comment
'*stay together*'

Bob.
**(booming like father xmas,
whilst taking a sip of
whiskey).**

Ha ha ha ha, stay together,
that's a good un

Martin.

With me being a computer
buff, and the fact she
already had a six foot
hunk of a fireman, my
chance of any action

Martin. Cont'd.

was rather diminished……..

If only I hadn't chucked
the cuff keys in the sea,
prior to getting to the
night club things could
have been so much easier

Bob.
(sipping his latte with
crossed legs and picking
up the times newspaper).

Dumbs follow blondes

Gus.
(standing up and gyrating
back and forth this time).

Could have done her puppy
dog style you spacka, like
they do in the movies, if
she had her back to you
like that, that is

Martin.

Yeah, 'n if you'd been a
fireman I'd have brought
her back here for you

Martin. Cont'd.

Beavis, and watched from close quarters but se la vie monsieur, se la vie

Gus.

You cock chimp, you could've lied to her

Martin.

Tried it Dez, but she wanted the uniform mate

Darrell.
(looking at Wibble and shaking his head).

What time does the bar open son?

Michael.
(checking his watch and wiping it, as it's smeared in relish).

We found 'Spoon's opens at 10am, so 20 minutes scrub up and in we go

Steve.
(arising).

If you are gunna be a
squaddie be the SAS, chop,
chop lads, we might miss
valuable drinking time if
we don't hurry up

Carl.
(winking at his nemesis).

Be a shame to sober up,
we're top of the food
chain, but are rather
fond of drink instead

Bob.

Agreeing impartially young
brother, that it would,
lead the way

14. INT. Walking out of   **14**
      Restaurant. Cont'd

Darrell.
(looking at the twins).

You two been at it all
night again?

Carl.

Kind of Dip, the YTS lad was just closing the bar at 1.30 when we got in, so we gave him £200 to stay with us for the evening

Darrell.

Good call chicken's, what time did you let him leave?

Bob.

He put his pinny on, served us brekky and then parted ways

Darrell.

Wibble, why didn't we think of that lad?

Michael.

Lanky, judging by the dilapidated condition of our room, we were in no fit state to quaff any further alcoholic beverages,

Michael. Cont'd.

Christ my head's banging!,
you sure we only had
alcohol?

Darrell.

Fairly sure

Chopper is chuckling to himself
whilst walking along behind.

15. INT. Reception Cont'd   15

Michael.
(whispering).

Boys, hide me whilst we
walk past the receptionist
please

Carl.

Why?, and why is the
receptionist holding that
painting?

Michael.
(tucking in behind Gus).

Long story Chumpy, just
keep walking

Chopper chuckles again, shuffling
along behind.

Michael.

Boys, see you in 'Spoons in
ten, Daz hurry up we've
gotta get to the room
before the cleaner and give
it the once over

16. INT. Corridor   16
        Outside Bedroom. Cont'd.

Michael.
**(whispering as they
approach the room whilst
two cleaners stand
outside).**

Never mind, too late,
just walk past

Darrell.

Morning ladies

MAID.

Scum of the earth

Michael Sandoz

Darrell.
(peeking in the room).

Wow, ladies what kind of
person would do this and
then expect you two lovely
girls to clean it up?....
Shorty, come back here we
have some damsels in
distress who need our help

Mickey returns and tries to look
surprised, as they enter the room.

17.   INT. Bedroom.   17

Michael.
(helping tidy up).

Rock band in town?

PRETTIER MAID.
(wringing out Donny's
skids over the sink).

Dirty filthy bastards!

Michael.
(using a towel to remove
the shaving foam).

At least it's not wee wee

Daz shoots him a killer glare.

Prettier Maid.
(picking up some dank socks).

How do you know?

Michael.
(wiping the wall endlessly as the shaving foam stain won't go).

True, just a guess..I guess

Daz slides his hand across his neck to tell Mickey to shut up and he shuts up rapido.

Fade Out / Fade in
18. INT. Lecture Theatre   18
**   Oxford University.**

Professor CHRIS TURNER is lecturing to a theatre of 60 students. He's in his late 20's, not much older than his students, rugged, tall and trendy smart.

He has drawn on the big white board his idea's based upon historical evidence on what the Holy Grail could actually be.

**Chris Turner
(using a laser pointer)**

So summarising, simmer down
there at the back, we have
four plausible solutions,

A it's the holy chalice
used in the last supper,
B it's a vessel holding
Jesus's blood from the
cross,
C it's information
leading to the lineage of
Jesus Christ, and
D it's the gospel
written by Jesus himself

HAWTHORNE puts his hand up in the
audience.

Professor Chris Turner.

Yes Hawthorne

Hawthorne.

Or Professor Turner it's all
four?

Sniggers echo through the
auditorium. Hawthorne looks at
everyone wondering what he's said
wrong now.

Professor Chris Turner.

The chances of that
Hawthorne are similar to
you reaching the dizzy
heights of a 2.2

Objects are thrown at Hawthorne by
his contemporaries.

Professor Chris Turner.

Right, that's enough
frolics… we've already
discounted the suggestion
it's Christ's mummified
head, so this shouldn't
take you lot too long

Professor Chris Turner picks up
his things and heads for the exit.

Professor Chris Turner. Cont'd

I want your thesis on the
pros and cons of each
theory on my desk by 6
tonight

EMMA with doe eyes, breathes a big
sigh as he leaves the room.

Fade across

19. INT. Hotel bedroom   **19**
door way.
(Fifteen minutes later).

Darrell.
(sliding his hands together as if removing dust).

Didn't that go well?, who'd have thought we'd 've had help!

The maids hurry up the corridor to the next room thanking the boys time and time again.

Michael.

Teflon mate, fucking teflon, bring that bike Dip, I'll be kissed by a baboons arse if Donny's having that pound deposit back

Darrell.
(wheeling the bike into the corridor).

Least I can do, a small price to pay for such collateral damage

Fade Out / Fade in
20. INT. Chicks House   **20**

CALVIN   is   standing   in   his
underpants on the phone.

Calvin.

Doh, don't put the phone
down, it's me again I'm at
23 West Street, going to
'Spoons, how long for a
taxi?

The phone goes dead.

Calvin.

She's done it again, what's
wrong with these people?

CHICK.
(standing in the kitchen
doorway).

Never mind my little roman
solider.. toast?

Calvin.

Go on then

Chick.

Then sex?

Calvin.

I'll be spoiling you again

Chick.

Spoil away

Fade across

21.   INT. Hotel Reception   21
          Cont'd.

Darrell.

You head on Porg, I need to
get our room changed,
there's no way I'm sleeping
in that mess again tonight

Michael.

Alright son, see you in a
mo', shall I take the bike?

Darrell.
(shooing him away).

No it's all in good hands
son, you go on

Darrell wanders over to the reception desk as Mickey heads out of the revolving doors.

Darrell.

Good morning sweetheart, I'd like to make a complaint about our room, we found it in a shocking state

Receptionist.
(looking for somewhere to put down the painting).

Really sir?, we really do hold our presentation in high regard, but if you definitely aren't happy, I can offer you another room?

Darrell.

That would be a good start

Receptionist.
(looking at the room bookings).

Let me just look to see what we have...hmmm....

Receptionist. Cont'd.

oh dear we seem to be out of
rooms sir, we only have the
bridal suite left but we
know that a wedding is
arriving, and they appear,
in the midst of all their
preparations, to have
forgotten to book it, so we
are reserving it

Darrell.

If my rooms not changed, we
will not only not be
paying, but I will ensure
my other guests don't pay
either

**Receptionist.
(looking up at him and
clicking the keyboard).**

Hmmm, that's all done sir,
can I have your key?

Darrell hands her his key, she
hands him the bridal suite key.

Darrell.

Thank you for your help

Receptionist.

My pleasure sir, enjoy your stay

Daz wheels the bike to the front door and heads off to the bike shelter. Upon reaching the bike shelter, he puts the bike back and gets the £1 deposit, he spins it up in the air, and heads off to the nearest newsagent.

Entering the newsagents Daz goes to the counter and buys a scratch card. He wins £300.

The shop assistant checks the card and gets £300 out of the till. She hands Daz the money.

Darrell.
(to the shop assistant, whilst waving the money in the air).

That, my dear, is karma

He walks out.

Fade out / Fade in

22. INT. Chicks House   22

Calvin is on the phone again. The Chick is in the kitchen doorway looking more dishevelled.

Calvin.

Is that someone different, oh thank the lord, please please don't put the phone down, all I know is where I am and where I want to go, and I need to be there urgently or the boys will fine me………..23 West St, you will?, super

Chick.

How long?

Calvin.

10 mins

Chick.

Sex?

Calvin

You don't know how lllucky you are…..

Fade Out / Fade in
23.   INT. 'Spoons – Pub – Day   23

Mickey enters 'Spoons and seeing
Carl at the bar, walks over

Carl.

Hair of the dog DB?

Michael.

Might as well Chumpy, only
here once and you're only
fifty once…. get Dipper one
as well

Carl.
(handing him a beer).

Good lad, what kept you?

Michael.
(pulling a half turtle).

Donny's skids

Carl looks at him blankly.

Michael. Cont'd.

I'll spare you the details

Carl.
(swigging his beer as
though it's the first of
the day).

Ohhh, ohh, oh, that is like honey to a bee

Chopper chuckles in his nearly empty first pint overhearing the conversation.

Chopper, aka Stevie Rickham, the finest golfer in the world, (off seven anyway) gets up and heads for the bar.

Steve.
(addressing the boys).

Same again my inebriated compatriots?

Gus.
(raising his glass).

As it's a fine day Chopper me lad

Martin.

If I must keep up

Bob.
**(lifting his glass of 15
year old scotch and smoking
a huge Cuban cigar
scrounged off the YTS lad a
couple of hours earlier
whilst rocking back in his
faux leather armchair).**

Would be a shame not to,
get me a Savannah also,
this Cuban tastes stale

Mickey having barely left the bar
re-joins Chopper.

Michael.

You got his wallet son?

Steve.
**(catching the barmaids
attention).**

Yeah, funny ain't it?

Michael.

Hell is it funny Chopper,
when he gets here he's
gunna tear you to shreds

Michael Sandoz

Steve.

Yeah funny ain't it, not as
funny as the mattress trick
though, seven lagers and a
Savannah please, we tipped
Daz on the floor put his
mattress on top of you and
slid your mattress from
underneath you with
military precision and
neither of you woke up….
That's talent son….

Couldn't have done it
without my brief at my side
though, it helps to have a
solicitor present in case
things go tit's up

Oh, and the burger, that
was Dez's idea before you
hit me. Use his half eaten
burger as a pillow!.
Mustard!

The barmaid drops seven lagers in
front of Stevie and hands him the
Savannah.

Barmaid.

If he smokes this one I'll
shove it up his arse

Michael.
(picking something yellow
from his right ear).

Mustard, you hit that
on the nail……. so how'd
you get in the room?

Steve.

Ahh, we sorted that trick
out in the curry house,
swapped card keys with Daz
without him knowing, you
know how he always puts
his possessions on the
table instead of leaving
them in his pocket, the
dumb numbskull?

Michael.

Arhh..that would explain
why Daz's key wouldn't
work, asking for trouble
with you two consummate
professionals around. Oh
well then, the Dipper got
what the Dipster deserved,
when you giving him the
wallet back?

Steve.
(chuckling and supping his second pint).

Might just string it out a bit longer

Michael.

Damage done now son, cards are cancelled, including the wife's!

Steve.

Ouch, that's gunna smart

Michael.

Might as well give it back when he arrives, you can sub him too for the rest of the trip as he can't get any wonga

Steve.

Shi.. orly not , that was quick?

Michael.

Tell me about it, it was my suggestion too, so now he's

Michael. Cont'd.

gunna think I was in on it,
I can't take another one of
his punches this holiday my
stomach's already bruising,
look…

Mickey lifts his polo shirt up to
show of the ever darkening skin.

Dipper enters the pub to a fanfare
of cheers.

Steve.

Here he is, the victim of
crime!

Darrell.
(ignoring him).

Where's my pint pond
life's?, I've got some
celebrating to do

Michael.

Ordered you one Dip,
what you done with it
Chumpy?

Carl.
(finishing the glass off
in front of him and heading
to the bar).

Oh, Sorry Dip, was a tadge
thirsty, a pint of golden
shower on its way

Bob.
(raising his glass to an
echo of further and me and
me's).

Get me one too bro, with a
little chaser if the budget
will stretch that far

Gus.

As the suns up

Steve.

Would hate to go thirsty

Michael.

Slip one on the counter for
me too Chumpy

Martin.

Just a swifty

Darrell.
(staring horrified at his ringing phone).

This ain't good.. it's the wife, arhhh we're supposed to be on the golf course now, quieten down boys………….

Hiya sweetheart, yes fourth hole, yes quiet, just a few beers and a curry, in bed for 12, you're where?, the supermarket and the credit cards aren't working?. Haven't got a clue sweetheart, how are the kids, did you get a good night's sleep without chuckle bear to keep you warm?

Michael.

Fore right

Carl.
(louder).

Fore right

Darrell.

It's Mickey and Carl,
Mickey's just teed off and
hit it straight right at
some tourists walking to
the beach, must go it's my
shot next speak to you
later, bye, bye, bye, bye,
no you put the phone down
first, no the lads are
listening, alright, luv
you, bye, bye bye, see you,
bye bye bye

Carl.
**(sniggering in his twins
direction).**

'Chuckle Bear' Fat Bob,
he's gunna regret that one

Bob.
**(from behind the Times
newspaper as a cloud of
Savannah smoke arises from
the pages).**

That is for certain dear
Bro

Steve.

She alright Daz?

Darrell.
(with a worried look on his face).

Not really Chopper, in the supermarket with a £200 shopping trolley, three hungry kids and no cards are working, thieving bastard's… if I get my hands on the tea leafs they'll wish they'd never been born

Michael.
(turns and quietly whispers to Chopper).

Lose the wallet Stevie, lose the wallet

Steve.
(slipping it down the back of the chair).

On it

Michael.

Good lad, probably best if we don't mention it again

Gus.
(as Calvin saunters into the pub).

Ohh, look who it is, the Greek love god returns from his lair

Calvin.
(with a big beaming smile).

Hello boys, sorry I'm late, had to wait for a taxi for a couple of hours, how far behind am I?

Martin.

The twins or the rest of us?

Calvin.
(going for the safer option).

Errm, the rest of you Donny?

Martin.

Just the three Eros, shouldn't take you too long to catch up

Calvin.

Go get me three in then
Mickey boy, I just spent my
last three nicker on a taxi

Mickey goes to the bar.

Calvin.
(taking Mickey's seat).

Never guess what boy's,
I've just spent two hours
waiting for a taxi at this
chick's place, only for it
to eventually come after
fifteen phone calls, drive
200 yards down the road and
drop me off here!!

Darrell.
**(looking at Chopper with
a Wallace type grin).**

And we rely on people like
this to keep us safe?

Steve.

Could be worse could be
me?!

Eros gets back up and heads to the
bar to help Mickey who's ordered
six pints of lager.

Calvin.
(looking concerned).

Said three Wibble?

Michael.

Thought I'd join you

Calvin.

Fair do's Wib, always enjoy
a couple of three scoops
with me old mucka

Michael.
(crossing his leg up a
little and handing Calvin a
couple of twenties).

Arrh I'm bursting Cal, take
these twenties for the
beers Eros, I need a waz

Mickey heads off to the dunny in
rather a rush.

A bloke at the bar sits quietly watching him as he passes.

                Calvin.
        (taking the twenties and slipping them into his back pocket)......

Coming with you son... Daz, pay the good lady will you

                Darrell.
        (comes to the bar and clears the debt out of his hard earned £300).

Shorty left you high and dry again son?

                Calvin.
        (looking back with a sad look on his face).

He has Dip

24.   INT Men's WC. Urinals   24

                Calvin.
        (removing his tadger from his trousers and standing next to Mickey).

Another good night had by
all Wib

Michael.
(looking down).

Judging by the size of
that, I doubt she had much
fun Cal

Calvin.
(shaking the limp slug).

Very funny son, very funny,
it's just worn down,
friction me lad, it erodes
most things

Michael.
(looking startled).

Somehow Eros, that
I can believe.. n, n, no
way is that semen dribbling
from your bell end?

Calvin.
(staring a little closer
and shaking the string
of semen down the pan).

Oh would you look at that
DB, go on my little

fellers go forth and
multiply

**Michael.
(looking even more
concerned).**

Cal, is that brown stuff on
your bell what I think it
is?

**Calvin.
(proudly and loudly).**

Oh yes Shorty, go get me a
tissue from the throne will
you Wib

Mickey obliges and brings back
some loo paper.

Michael.

Cal, you'll catch something
riding bareback in the
pencil sharpener

Calvin.

Did my homework son, not
had sex in three years,

a clean one as they're
called in the trade

Michael.
(sarcastically).

How lucky was she!….
bumping into you then
matey?

Calvin.
(looking proud of his
night's work).

Very lucky son, and
there'll be more lucky,
lllucky ladies this evening

Calvin. Cont'd.
(handing Mickey the tissue
and zipping up his fly).

Stick this down the pan for
me will you Porg

Mickey obliges as Eros heads back
to the bar.

25.　INT. WC Cubicle　　　　25

Michael.
(under his breath whilst he
flushes the loo).

For that I am sure

26. INT. Bar. Cont'd   **26**

Darrell.
(as Eros swaggers back to the boys).

What you gone and done with the little fella Cal?

Carl.

Is he still looking for steps so he can reach the urinal?

Steve.

Or has he fallen in the pan again, son?

Calvin.
(as Mickey pushes the toilet door open unaware he is the butt of the joke).

He's just running a little errand

At the bar the bloke is talking
quietly on his phone.

He has ear phones in and is
sipping a triple bourbon.

GABRIEL.

> Has he got through yet?,
> are you having a laugh?,
> have you seen what you put
> him in?...first prototype?,
> are you shitting me, you
> sent the saviour of Earth
> down to Earth as a first
> prototype?, this just gets
> more comical by the minute,
> typical God, half-finished
> job…. No I don't want to
> talk to him right now, I'm
> feeling pretty angry and
> let down. D'you know, he is
> only able to get through
> when the mortal has had a
> gallon of ale?, and then
> for obvious reasons nobody
> listens to him……..what you
> laughing at?, just 'cause
> you ain't down here facing
> annihilation it doesn't
> make it funny…..Ok I'll
> check in tomorrow, things
> will be getting heated up

by then.. bye......... bunch of
fekking amateurs

Fade out / Fade in
27.   INT. Heathrow Airport   27
          Departure Lounge

The ARCHBISHOP OF CANTERBURY is
taking a call in departures.

He is putting his Raybans on, and
is holding a bottle of beer.

The   departure   gate   shows
Fiumicino,   Leonardo   da   Vinci
International Airport.

Archbishop of Canterbury.

> I know it's dangerous, but
> if the rumours are true,
> I have to do it, it might
> be my last chance of
> visiting

BISHOP ON OTHER END OF PHONE.(OS)

> But why now Archbishop?,
> your subjects are here, they
> need you

Archbishop of Canterbury.

> It's a pilgrimage of sorts
> Bishop, you won't understand

Fade across:

28. EXT. Outside Professor   28
Chris Turners Flat

The Professor is standing outside his flat, he has a coffee in one hand, paper in the other and a Danish pastry stuck in his mouth.

He puts the Danish pastry onto the paper using his mouth, but still realises he can't get to his keys.

Professor Chris Turner.

> Come on Turner, and you think you can find the holy grail, you can't even work out how to open your front door

He puts the paper down gets his keys out and opens the door.

As he enters he sees a message on his answer phone and press's it as he passes.

CHRIS'S MOM.

Hi darling, mommy here, haven't heard from you for a while, you found yourself a lovely lady yet?

Professor Chris Turner.

Would help if I knew what I liked first mom

Chris's Mom.

Me and daddy are thinking of coming up at the weekend, if you're free give us a call, byeee

Professor Chris Turner.

Brill my week just got better

He knocks his shoes off, and heads to his bedroom taking his clothes off.

Fade across

29.   INT. 'Spoons – Pub – Day   29
              Cont'd

Martin.

Lads, we can't sit here
quaffing all day, there's a
world to explore out there
            Carl.
(looking at his twin).

Can't we?

Bob stares back with a mirror
image expression of surprise and
confusion.

            Martin.
**(standing up, necking half
a pint and heading for the
door).**

Come on, sup up, let's go
'n do the pitch and putt
to waste a couple of hours

            Bob.
**(getting up and stubbing
the Savannah out).**

Waste a couple of hours?,
since when has drinking
wasted a couple of hours?

            Darrell.
**(talking to Gus whilst
heading to the exit).**

Did we have a vote on this Dezmond?, you know ballot boxes, little pieces' of paper…tick?

Gus.

It's clearly not a democracy today Dipper

Steve.
(trudging behind).

Not entirely sure I'm into totalitarian rule

Michael.
(from just behind).

You love it Chopper, and don't try to deny it…… didn't you get married?

Martin.

Wibble what was that you were saying about time last night?

Michael.

That drinking wasn't
wasting a couple of hours
Donny?

Martin.

No, that Einstein messed up
with his variable time
theory, getting above your
station here aren't you?

Darrell.

I thought that Chimp, the
atomic clock proved time is
variable

Michael.

Not really boys, time has
three meanings that have
been intertwined, we have
what I call as real time

This is time that moves
constantly from now to the
future, creating the past

We have physical time, time
that is relative to our
motion around the sun,
years and days

And we also have man made time consisting of months, hours, minutes and seconds

Steve.

You appear to have had too much time on your hands Wibble

Michael.

So, when you look at the three options you can see that Einstein dumped his theory into man made time, rather than physical time which is relative to aging

Carl.

Why can't it be put into real time Mickey me lad?

Michael.

Can you imagine living in that world Carl, speed up slow down, stop

Calvin.

Sounds a bit like the instructions from my last conquest

Michael.

Life would be a confusing mess, no real time ticks on constantly, never changing

The boys are at the car getting their putters and wedges from the car boot.

Calvin.

Like the sound of that world though Wib, could kick a bad one out of bed quicker when the time arises, or stop time if she's a peach

Bob.

Why is physical time relative to aging DB?

Michael.

Well in physical time we have years and days and that's what we use to age ourselves, so when Einstein said one clock slowed down, it didn't actually slow down, it aged slower

Steve.

Not quite sure I follow Wibble

Michael.

So by travelling faster or slower aging changes not time

Calvin.

How fast do I have to go then Wib, to keep these good looks constant?

The boys get to the pitch and putt and pay the assistant whist still discussing time.

Michael.

Well aging is a wave Eros, so take your pick, just like light waves, sound

waves, radio waves and
microwaves, aging varies
with speed and is a wave

Gus.

Told you going too fast in
my wheels was good for me

Steve.

And my mom told me to stay
off the stuff

Michael.

Not that sort of speed
Chopper, I mean velocity

Bob.

Arhh yes velocity is rate
and direction of travel

Michael.

Nice one Bob, so we have
the Earth rotating, as it
rotates around the sun,
and the sun is moving and
rotating in relation to the
milky way and the milky way
is moving and rotating in

relation to the universe,
all that equals aging on
Earth at 90ish years

Martin.

That would explain genesis
Wib, always wondered how
Noah lived for 900 years

Michael.

It does, it explains it
very well Donny, all God
had to do was slow the
Earth's rotation down
and bingo we all lived
shorter lives

Darrell.

You keep mentioning God
Wib?

The thought of a master
controller up there in the
ethos sends chills down my
spine

Steve.

Imagine living under the dictatorship of a Chimp for 900 years Daz, just this morning's been bad enough

Carl.

We'd never be short of banana's though Chopper

Calvin.

And swinging would be high on the agenda, if you pardon the expression

Michael.

And you'd have a complete harem of ladies under your control Eros

Calvin.

Tell me something new Wib, lucky llucky harem they are

30. **EXT. Southport Pitch and   30
     Putt 1st Tee.**

The boys are now standing on the first tee, undertaking various forms of warm up routines.

Calvin.

Let's get this holiday started

Michael.

That was it Calvin, where man went wrong, when god created the Earth he did the lot in six days, rested on the seventh, and the eighth day was supposed to be the holy – day or holiday as we know it. With eight days to the week man has much more productivity, and much more time to spend with family and pursuits

Calvin.

You might have gone wrong Wib, I went into fire-fighting in full knowledge of the 4 days on 4 days off work ethic, been telling you all for years, makes things a lot more simple to have affairs

Steve.

All for the wrong reasons as usual

Darrell.
(teeing up as though it is his God given right to go first).

Right, there's no time like the present to fill my pockets with pleasant, fiver a corner boys and I'm not accepting peanuts today Chimp, got kids to feed

Eight holes later the boys have reached the ninth, as Daz tees up two shots in the lead.

31. EXT. Southport Pitch   31
and Putt 9ᵗʰ Tee.

On the adjacent tee, only 10 yards away, Donny spots someone he thinks he knows.

Martin.

Christ boys is that Gene Wilder on the 7ᵗʰ Tee?

Gus.

No, it's Rednapp you
spacka Chimp

Martin.

So it is

He shouts over to Harry.

Martin.

Jamie, you've aged since
your playing days

Harry walks over.

Harry.

I think you're mistaking
me for my handsome son, but
I'll take any compliment
these days

Martin.

Ohh it's the manager lads
not the pundit, Harry is
there any chance of a
photo?

Harry.

Certainly Lads

Donny gets his phone out of his pocket and hands it to Harry.

The boys all pose whilst Harry, in complete bemusement, takes the photo.

Martin.
(taking the camera back).

Cheers Harry, wait till I tell everyone at home you took that photo

Darrell. Cont'd.
(whilst lining up a 90 yard wedge shot like a two foot putt).

Tenner off each of you if this goes in.. Porg, get the brownies off the boys will you, I'm busy, you know what it's like getting the money off this lot after the event

As Mickey collects the brownies
from the dumbstruck half dozen,
Daz practices his highly tuned
celebrity swing, and steps up to
the ball.
He majestically swings at the
ball, striking it beautifully, it
lands, two bounces in!!.

Daz does a Hale Irwin down to the
hole and back, bringing back the
ball and kissing it whilst taking
the brownies out of Mickey's hand.

Darrell.

Woohooo...

Darrell. Cont'd.

I started the day robbed
Wibble me son and that's
£405 now. I might start
this as a living scamming
you lot, follow that Chimp!

Donny tees up and shanks it
straight over the adjacent road.
The ball hits a car and it bounces
back and lands in a bush, to which

seven kind and caring mates fall around on the floor laughing.

In a fit of temper Donny snatches Mickey's ball out of his hand, tees up and cans it on the fly.

Martin.
(as the boys fall silent).

Stick that down as a three

Calvin.

Wibble, if you can follow that and get it in the hole I will let you suck my willy later after I have dipped it in tonight's spoils

Bob.
(looking at his twin).

There's an offer

Carl.
(nodding).

Punani flavoured Saveloy, mmmmmmm

Gus.

Tasted worse

Michael's searching for his ball, gives up and quietly slips his hand into Carls pocket and takes a ball out.

Michael.

> You don't know where it's been boys, but I'm not one to back out of a challenge like that

Michael address's the ball and makes a swing. The ball rises high in the air and slam dunks straight into the hole, bounces out and stops on the edge.

Mickey goes wild.

Michael.
**(emulating Daz's Hale Irwin impression without much success, running down towards the hole and looking more like a dwarf on Prozac).
Screaming**...

> It's my lucky night!,

Woa ho ho ho….

Calvin.

Get out of here, the ball's
not in the hole!
Gus.

To be fair Eros, you only
said get it in the hole,
and we all saw it go in the
hole didn't we boys, you
said fuck all about it
having to stay in the hole

Steve.

I'm happy to second that

Calvin.
(deciding not to argue).

Wibble, I was only jesting
son, you don't have to
if you don't want to

Michael.
(continuing Eros's woes and
down on the green).…

I'll get some chocolate
spread from little
Tecko's on the way back
lover boy… at least it

> will taste better then

Chopper tees up still laughing uncontrollably and snap hooks it straight left towards the pay hut where four Japanese tourists are bartering with the attendant.

> **Martin.**
> **(shouting and slightly**
> **worried for his Eastern**
> **counterparts)....**

> FORE RIGHT!

The ball whittles between the tourists, skims the attendant's ear, hits the back wall and lands back in the ball basket.

Silence falls on the lads and the five dumbstruck people standing sixty yards away, as they all turn to look at Donny.

> **Daz.**
> **(in total astonishment).**

> Fore right?

> **Carl.**

(shaking his head)

Fore right Chimp?

    Steve.
(looking around at the
Chimp and feeling rather
lucky he hasn't just killed
someone).

Fore fekking right?

        Gus.
(checking his hands just to
make sure).

That's fore left you spacka!

        Martin.
(looking puzzled).

But that's what they all
shout at our local
municipal golf course?

        Steve.
(shaking his head).

That's because they're all
shit golfers Donny, and can
only slice the ball right

        Martin.

Ohhh,…. didn't think it made any sense, so if it goes left we shout fore left then?

Darrell.

Would you listen to Einstein over there, I think that's a cue to get back to the safety of the pub lads before we have funeral to frequent this afternoon

Calvin.
(putting his ball back in his pocket).

Yeah, all for that, should be some talent in there now

Carl nods approvingly whilst searching all his pockets for his ball, but finding something much better in his back pocket.

Bob.
(to the skinnier brother).

How can you better those
five shots youngster?,
come on we're wasting
valuable drinking time here

Carl.
(pulling a small bottle of
vodka from his rear pocket,
unscrewing the cap and
taking a large gulp).

You might be Clutch

Darrell.

Get a shifty on Shorty!, we
need to listen to some more
of your 'St Michael,
Warlord of the Saints'
bull shit you start
spouting after 8 pints, it
keeps us all entertained
for hours

Michael.
(lining up his two foot
putt and taking numerous
practice strokes).

I do what?

The boys have gone without him.

Michael. Cont'd.

```
    Wait, wait for me boys,
    WAIT!!,  Daz, stick that
    down as a two son, boys
    slow down
The boys head on regardless.
```

Fade out

```
        --
        --
        --
        --
```

End

ABOUT THE AUTHOR

Michael Sandoz is a lifelong Electrical Engineer.

He's feeling very lucky he hasn't killed anyone over the years, but most importantly himself, not due to his engineering prowess but situations he keeps getting himself caught up in, many of which will be played out in these episodes.

His first experience with electricity was as an eight year old when he decided to remove the bulb from his bedside lamp and put his fingers where the prongs were.

He survived, but did a full somersault over the bed.

He has spent the past 19 years trying to be that sensible person, due to his children, and even then should possibly have died half a dozen times.

How many people have stood behind someone at an airport check in who has a gun in their luggage?

It's just Mickey isn't it?......

It's been hard, very hard, and now at the age of 49 he
has decided growing up has kind of passed him by.

A few years ago, his youngest daughter requested a
'See Spot Run Daddy' in his place.

Feeling hurt…very hurt he has recreated himself as a
super hero.

The biggest super hero of all time……

The man tasked with creating Peace on Earth.

-

-

I bet it still won't be good enough.

Michael Sandoz

This novel is a work of fiction and is the product of the author's imagination, inspired by the author's life and experiences and points of view.

Some real events, incidents, places, people and works of art or music have been mentioned or described but are used fictitiously